THE ORANGE DOVE OF FIJI

POEMS FOR THE WORLD WIDE FUND FOR NATURE

THE ORANGE DOVE OF FIJI

Poems for the World Wide Fund for Nature

Edited by
Simon Rae

Preface by
H.R.H. The Duke of Edinburgh

Hutchinson
London   Sydney   Auckland   Johannesburg

The poets and artists represented in this book have donated their work without receiving a fee, and all royalties are to be paid to the World Wide Fund for Nature.

This book is printed on recycled paper.

This edition first published in 1989 by
Hutchinson

© in this collection The World Wide Fund for Nature 1989

The © in individual poems and illustrations remains with the poet and artist

Century Hutchinson Ltd, Brookmount House,
62–65 Chandos Place, London WC2N 4NW

Century Hutchinson Australia (Pty) Ltd
20 Alfred Street, Milsons Point, Sydney, NSW 2061

Century Hutchinson New Zealand Limited
PO Box 40–086, Glenfield, Auckland 10, New Zealand

Century Hutchinson South Africa (Pty) Ltd
PO Box 337, Bergvlei, 2012 South Africa

Phototypeset in Linotron Palatino by Input Typsetting Ltd, London
Printed and bound in Great Britain by
Courier International Ltd, Tiptree, Essex

British Library Cataloguing in Publication Data
The Orange dove of Fiji: poems for the worldwide Fund for Nature.
1. Poetry in English, 1945–. Special subjects.
Nature. Anthologies
I. Rae, Simon
821'.008'036

ISBN 0–09–173950–0

CONTENTS

* £1,000 *prize-winning poem*

ILLUSTRATIONS

BUCKINGHAM PALACE.

Poetry can reach parts of the mind that simple facts and statistics cannot reach. The will to conserve our fellow plant and animal inhabitants of this planet depends on two things; an understanding of the problems and a commitment to do what is necessary to solve them. The facts are easily established, it needs the language of the poet to stimulate commitment.

The contributors to this book of poems will have made a significant contribution to the conservation of nature if the readers are inspired to join the struggle to save the life of our planet from human folly and indulgence.

1989

ACKNOWLEDGEMENTS

This book would simply not have come into existence without the warm enthusiasm of Ivan Hattingh and Peter Martin of the World Wide Fund for Nature; the initial encouragement I received from poet friends; and the high degree of commitment shown by Tony Whittome of Century Hutchinson. I would also like to thank all the poets from whom I went on to solicit poems. With so many requests for unremunerated contributions, their response demonstrated a heartening degree of interest and generosity. David Hockney gave us permission to use 'Nichols Canyon' on the cover of the book, and the artists who have so beautifully illustrated some of the poems, gave their work free like the poets.

I would also like to thank Alan Rusbridger and Ian Mayes, the editors of the *Weekend Guardian*, for supporting the national poetry competition run as the second strand of the project. This was very successful, with over four thousand entries, and I would like to thank every one of the entrants, who not only collectively produced a high overall standard but also contributed materially to the WWF's funds. My thanks also go to Michael Baldwin, Ted Hughes and Peter Redgrove, who judged the competition, and to Nicky Palmer of WWF, who processed the entries so efficiently. Others who have given freely of their time to help the project forward include Lawrence Sail, John Whitworth and John Caperon. Finally, I owe thanks to my wife, the artist Penelope Rippon, who, having had the original idea, left me to get on with it.

Acknowledgements are due to the following publications: *Departures*, *Poetry Review*, the *Weekend Guardian*.

'Breach' by Alan Brownjohn, was taken from his *Collected Poems*, (Century Hutchinson), 'Neighbours' by Gillian Clarke, from *Letting in the Rumour* (Carcanet), 'The Cow *Perseverance*' by Fred D'Aguiar, from *Airy Hall* (Chatto and Windus), 'The Orange Dove of Fiji' by James Fenton, from *Manila Envelope* (Philippines), 'Bog' by John Fuller, from *The Secret Garden* (The Unidentified Flying Printer), 'Art & Extinction' by Tony Harrison, from *Selected Poems* (Penguin), 'Long Lines from the Island' by A. E. Markham, from *Towards The End of a Century* (Anvil), 'The Inheritor' by Gerda Mayer, from *The Knockabout Show* (Chatto and Windus), 'On Sizewell Beach' by Blake Morrison, from *The Ballad of the Yorkshire Ripper* (Chatto and Windus), and 'Site 792N/57' by Anthony Thwaite, was taken from *Poems 1953–1988* (Century Hutchinson).

Simon Rae

INTRODUCTION

The corrective hand of nature, which within the next fifty years will raise the temperature of the world by two or three degrees, and the level of the oceans by fourteen inches, brings us these poems.

Some of them were invited from known poets, some written in response to a competition sponsored by the World Wide Fund for Nature and the *Weekend Guardian*. The entries, including some strongly engaged pieces by children, confront the issues in ingenious ways.

The overall standard of entry was high, and selection difficult. In the event, our choice of prizewinners was unanimous.

MICHAEL BALDWIN
TED HUGHES
PETER REDGROVE

Elisabeth Frink

THE ORANGE DOVE OF FIJI

POEMS FOR THE WORLD WIDE FUND FOR NATURE

Granam Arnold

DANNIE ABSE

A Wall

in a field in the County of Glamorgan.
You won't find it named in any guidebook.
It lies, plonk, in the middle of rising ground,
forty-four paces long, high as your eyes,
it begins for no reason, ends no place.
No other walls are adjacent to it.
Seemingly unremarkable, it's just there,
Stones of different sizes, different greys.

Don't say this wall is useless, that the grass
on the shadow side is much like the other.
It exists for golden lichens to settle,
for butterflies in their obstacle race
chasing each other to the winning post,
for huddling sheep in a slanting rainfall,
for you to say, 'This wall is beautiful.'

FLEUR ADCOCK

The Last Moa

Somewhere in the bush, the last moa
is not still lingering in some hidden valley.
She is not stretching her swanlike neck
(but longer, more massive than any swan's)
for a high cluster of miro berries,
or grubbing up fern roots with her beak.

Alice McKenzie didn't see her
among the sandhills at Martin's Bay
in 1880 – a large blue bird
as tall as herself, which turned and chased her.
Moas were taller than seven-year-old
pioneer children; moas weren't blue.

Twenty or thirty distinct species –
all of them, even the small bush moa,
taller than Alice – and none of their bones
carbon-dated to less than five centuries.
The sad, affronted mummified head
in the museum is as old as a Pharoah.

Not the last moa, that; but neither
was Alice's harshly grunting pursuer.
Possibly Alice met a takahe:
the extinct bird that rose from extinction
in 1948, near Te Anau.
No late reprieve, though, for the moa.

Her thigh-bones, longer than a giraffe's,
are lying steeped in a swamp, or smashed
in a midden, with her unstrung vertebrae.
Our predecessors hunted and ate her,
gobbled her up: as we'd have done
in their place; as we're gobbling the world.

MICHAEL BALDWIN

The Leveller

One in St Margaret's
Being cut by my barrel-bellied friend who was jovial
About cutting trees; so he cut it,
A firm-footed beech, by fingers, toes, thumbs
And several good thwacks in the heart;
Soon after was admitted to hospital himself
To lose several branches -
I remember that one, and an elm with the beetle.

Then there was Beauty's garden
The week when the Beast was it died -
No, the Beast lived on: I mean the Prince
Or the King, the man kissing wine, pissing stars
And now bundled under the tall buds of Spring -
And Beauty growing tearful
Could not stand her forest where the Miracles
    had chased her,
Each Beauty, each Beast, in their four-footed maze,
So gave me a saw and an axe
And bade me chop them down.
The plums came first, and after the greengages,
Then five little nuts. As I chopped
Beauty watched me, as she did so
Growing older, growing ugly,
But ah! what of me?

There was one full of birds, not their bodies, their
    voices:
I chopped down birds a hundred trees high,
I chopped down the sun, I chopped down the Spring
Like a butcher with a chicken
I chopped as she bade me from each branch in Heaven

Little fruits little nuts struck from God in my season
Then walked home weeping with my legs in my hand.

3

CHRIS BENDON

Dipping Into the Rev. Wood's New Illustrated Natural History, Engraved by the Brothers Dalziel After Weir, Wolf, Zwecker etc

I catch a *Walking Fish* out for a stroll,
a cold *Fishing Frog's* look of malice -
it's pure Alice, these fish-on-plates' selfconscious
    expressions,
many with memorial borders, the whole spectrum
    implied
by black and white, life-sizes too reduced to fit
the spine's hide arc. A once new knower's ark,
inscribed *HMS Dolphin 1889*, except
(principle of decline and entropy) only, as a rule,
one of each kind. Which includes:

the *Ounce, Peeshoo, Daesman, Aswail,*
Narica, Ratel, Sondell, Pen-Tail,
Malayan Sun-Bear, and the *Radiated Mole.*

The *Agouti* and the *Taguan Flying Squirrel,*
the *Tortoiseshell* or *Smaller Clouded Tiger,*
the *Hackee,* the *Jelerang,* the *Prairie Dog* or *Wish-Ton-Wish,*
and, together with the King of Beasts, the *Jaguar*
    whose skin is
'very highly valued, being worth rather more than
three pounds . . . used for coverings of officers'
    saddles',
the *Wolverine,* 'more popularly known by the name of
    the *Glutton',*
the *Bison,* in 'multitudes . . . even now hardly
    diminished',
whose hump 'gives to the animal's back so strange an
    aspect'
for which 'hunters will often slay . . . leaving the
    remainder . . .

4

to the wolves and birds', the *Spring Haas* or *Cape Leaping Hare*,
the *Riet-Bok*, which, writes Col. Drayson, 'lies concealed
in the reeds . . . until he is nearly trodden on',
who 'stops to turn and look at his pursuers',
who 'will frequently gallop very freely
after a bullet has passed through his body',
the *Eland, Argali*, and *Aoudad*,
the *Nylghau* 'employed in the manufacture of shields',
the *Babyroussa*, the *Wallachian Sheep.*

Sloan's Rhinoceros and the *Rhinaster*
('the best place to aim is just behind the shoulder'),
the *Phatagin, Ant-Bear* or *Tamanoir* . . .

All patiently captured, either lightly or heavily
engraved; an empire with changes of name
and state, now-ness of 'now' become
then-ness of Then, this 'New' Natural History turned
past historic, the light of Genesis ever rising
                                    ever setting . . .

Next, the Birds of Paradise or simple heavens
for which (pre-Freud) 'not so easy to avoid
a considerable sameness in the language . . .
The words green, scarlet, black and white
necessarily occur so frequently . . .':
Superb Plume Bird, Beautiful Trogon,
here's *Gould's Neomorpha*, the *Little Flame Bearer*,
which, 'as Mr Gould happily remarks,
seems to have caught the last spark
from the volcano (Chiriqui)
before it was extinguished . . .',
the *Rifle Bird, Lammergeyer, Esculent Swallow*,
the *Jer-Falcon* and the *Passenger Pigeon*,
its 'multitudes . . . several miles in (sic) breath',
Darter, Greak Auk, Adjutant, and *Magpie*,
'the pert, the gay, the mischievous'.

Then, in Lepidoptera, Moths:
Hawks *Oleander* and *Hylas Bee*,
catocala fraxinus, or *Clifden Nonpareil*,
'the largest British species of genus'
(certainly without comparison in the modern *Observer*),
the *Longhorn*, the *Codling*, the *Goat*, the *Death's Head*,
and fluttering, feathery, surrendered *White Plume*.

Among Beetles, the *Chrysochroa's* 'fiery copper',
a 'native of India . . . burnished blue' like
'a well-tempered watch-spring'.

Mole-Cricket, Ant-Lion, Nemoptera Coa.

Glass Snake, Lettered and *Chicken* Tortoises,
the *Moloch, Horned Frog* and *Matamata* . . .

And so back to the sea again, for
'seventy gallons of clear and scentless oil'
from the *Sea Elephant*, 'trembling . . . like masses of
    jelly',
for *Cuvier's Bodian, Oreosoma*, and *Lyrie*,
for *Jew-Fish*, aliases *Stone Basse, Wreck Fish, Couch's
    Polyprion*,
John Dory, whose 'changing tints . . . rapidly vanish
    after death',
for *White Shark*, 'finny pirate of the ocean',
for *Horned Trunk-Fish* and *Belted Horseman*,
Becuna, whose scales provide 'minute crystalline
    spiculae . . .
useful in . . . preparation of artificial pearls'
but whose flesh is 'well-favoured and often brought to
    table',
for *Lump Fish*, 'frequently seen in the Scotch markets
    . . . second only to the *Turbot*'. And
'Everyone has heard of the *Sucking Fish* . . .
reported to adhere to the bottom of ships . . .
to arrest their progress . . . as if they had struck

a rock. Even after death, or when the disc is separated
   from

the body, this curious organ can be applied
to any smooth object and will hold
with tolerable firmness.' So, next,

Molluscs: the *Staircase* or *Perspective Trochus*,
the *Marbled Chiton*, the *Shell-Collecting Phorus*,
Doris, Doto, Cleodora,
the *Panther Cowry*, and the Glaucus,
the Hammer-Shell, and *Violet Snail*,
Ship Worm, Sea Trumpet, Spined Neritina.

Last, and first, so not least,
algae, plankton, weeds and shrimps . . .
the *Physalis* jellyfish, over whose body
a 'general iridescence . . . topaz, sapphire and
   aquamarine
   . . . plays', *Medusae* 'passing in shoals through . . .
      clear water,
pulsating as if the whole being were but
a translucent heart, rolling gently over

   as if in excess
   of happiness . . .

And some of these creatures luminous, luminous.
And some of them never discovered, discoloured,
their hues never entering Wood's dense forest,
where 'the aid of colour is almost needed
to enable the reader
to realise the full vividness'.

   His rainbow though . . .

   silver-white
   vermilion
   carmine

rich scarlet
ruddy red
rose pink
pinky brown
mahogany
rich chestnut
chocolate
fiery orange
brilliant yellow
sulphur
golden green
lime
olive
apple
dazzling azure
dark blue
violet
church purple

and, between the extremes of black and white,

many other shades overlooked or neglected.

Finally, black darkness of

night-
lamp-
jetty-
ink-

-of coal, Ur-original *Tree*
from whence
the Ark, the Cross, and Paper, paper

. . . *engraved by the Brothers Dalziel,*
after *Weir, Wolf, Zwecker* etc.

ALISON BRACKENBURY

Going out

Nature does not exist. Dissolve him, her, it
into water, air; into a hillock
of rough, dead grass where the winter ponies stand
matted with mud, manes beating in their eyes.
You can see them from the road. If you walk close
they will smell you on the wind. You meet their eyes,
bright as stones on your fingers; more lustrous than
  your own.

As you walk back, stumbling over molehills
(the moles have left circles and chains of fresh black
  earth
scarring the field. What does this mean?) you see
a single dandelion. Spinning with green, it pushes
through February's damp air, while the ponies cough
for spring. Next light, the track is rock from frost.

There is waste; more waste. The dandelion's seeds
would have ridden the roads and the valleys of air
fallen on stone, the ponies' blank manes,
fallen on frost. Do not be confused
when thaw softens ruts, when the moles raise again
their unfinished circle, the shotguns blast
light birds from hard air. Nature is an excuse,

spits the gipsies' blaze by the bristling wood,
quickly disturbing the badgers' slow night.
Trespassers upon parcelled land
with old cars, tall children, they build up their fire,
a snapping stream through the raw afternoon.
Washing hangs, tethered, unable to blow.
Where is our summer, the fine heads, the silver
noons of long grass? The sparks fade. The sparks glow.

ALAN BROWNJOHN

Breach

Within a mile of a sea, which could be heard,
On a Chesterfield much too narrow,
On a night that was much too short,
These two achieved a rare sort of victory:

They carried through a completely unselfish,
Unkind-to-no-other-people act of love,
Between twelve twenty-seven and twelve
Forty-four, while the latest oil slick

Slurped at the sands in the dark.
Nightlong coastguards fought it with radioed
Data about its location, helicopters clattered
To neutralise the thing with chemical sprays,

And half the resort was out next morning, waiting
As for some dismal, predicted second coming.
But these two made their protest about
The general soilure of the world at the hands

Of the effortful and the crude by just one
Once-only, uncontrived breach
Of its chaos with love. And there should be
A plaque on the esplanade to this effect.

IAN CAWS

Fox

When I first saw the fox, lamplight prised flints
    from the wall like bottle tops. But
the fox was silent in a small country
while, over the roofs, there moved continents
of cloud. Three young cyclists missed his entry
    through the gates of the manor, plait-

ing themselves away down the road, and when
    I reached where he had been, I could
only pick my way through a stillness. Those
images remain, shining, and, between
my world and me, the fox still rests, neat as
    a gasket. And I hear him, crowd-

ed by the things in my night, barking me
    awake, in my territory
forever, as I now in his. With no
home, he seeks out mine in the dark and we
must live together, the fox and I, so
    strange yet helpless as history.

GILLIAN CLARKE

Neighbours

That spring was late. We watched the sky
and studied charts for shouldering isobars.
Birds were late to pair. Crows drank from the lamb's
  eye.

Over Finland small birds fell: song-thrushes
steering north, smudged signatures on light,
migrating warblers, nightingales.

Wing-beats failed over fjords, each lung a sip of gall.
Children were warned of their dangerous beauty.
Milk was spilt in Poland. Each quarrel

the blowback from some old story,
a mouthful of bitter air from the Ukraine
brought by the wind out of its box of sorrows.

This spring a lamb sips caesium on a Welsh hill.
A child, lifting her face to drink the rain,
takes into her blood the poisoned arrow.

Now we are all neighbourly, each little town
in Europe twinned to Chernobyl, each heart
with the burnt fireman, the child on the Moscow train.

In the democracy of the virus and the toxin
we wait. We watch for bird migrations,
one bird returning with green in its voice,

glasnost,
golau glas,
a first break of blue.

NOTE: *golau glas: blue light*

DAVID CONSTANTINE

Endangered Species

No wonder we love the whales. Do they not carry
Our warm blood below and we remember
Falling asleep in a feeling element
And our voices beating a musical way

To a larger kindred, around the world? Mostly
We wake too quickly, the sleep runs off our heads
And we are employed at once in the usual
Coveting and schemes. I was luckier today

And remembered leaving a house in the Dales
Like home for a night, the four under one roof,
I left them sleeping without a moon or stars
And followed my dreaming self along a road.

Daylight augmented in a fine rain.
I had the sensation of dawning on my face.
But for the animals (and they had gathered
The dark standing in fields and now appeared

Replete) the night dissolved, but in the light,
A grey-eyed light, under the draining hills
Some pools of woodland remained and in them owls
And beside my sleepwalking, along the borders

Owls accompanied me, they were echoing
From wood to wood, into the hesitant day
I carried the owls in their surviving wells
Of night-time. The fittest are a fatal breed

Perhaps. They would do without sleep if they could
And meter it for the rest of us. My kind
Have woodland in their open eyes all day.
They listen. I've seen them suddenly rapt by owls

From interrogations and at any moment
They'll quit a reasoning or a talking to
And dip their domes, their dreaming, hooting hills,
Down, down, into an infinite pacific.

WENDY COPE

Pine Forest

The track cuts through the forest
Like a parting. Between the trees
It's dark, a place for gnomes
And goblins. Near the ground
A snow of grey-white fungus
Lives on leafless wood.

'Just a little way,' you say
'Along this path.' Pine needles
Inches deep, an island of fresh grass
Where there is sun. We're whispering
As if we were in church.
Ahead of us the tunnel reaches
Into blackness. I take your hand.

MARTYN CRUCEFIX

Mikhael at Viksjön

They stopped bombing the lake with lime
a year ago. The helicopters stopped coming.
You see where it's unnaturally dark;
daylight vanishes undiminished to the bed.
I think of it as an absence of energy -
accepting everything and like the old
giving nothing back.

I hate them for it. The grey men who say
it's the British unfurling filthy flags,
blurting a language so strong it burns trees,
blackens the water, scalds memory clean
for a better world. Well, I've seen it:
I dreamed a sun above a dry, scuffed land
bleached white but for two mud-dark shelters,
lean-tos like wedges laid flat to the ground.
That was all. I tore every useless permit
I had, threw the scraps to the lake
wanting to see them shrivel into flame
as they touched the water.

I used to swim from the speckled rocks.
Swallows flashed above like fish through a lake.
First signs came with bright weather.
The water a lacklustre eye squeezed
under a skyline of pine like quills.
At the beach, the white bellies of perfect bream.

Then the helicopters waited till dusk
to drop their white loads crashing
and fizzing on the lake,
scrawling its surface like a mist.
Now they've stopped bombing and I no longer
think I see the tell-tale rings of rising fish.

Their splash would always hush the lake.
Now there is only a more difficult quiet,
one I use only for the anger which will not
follow the daylight to the bottom
but which comes clattering back at me off
the blackened water, louder and clearer,
louder and clearer!

NOTE
Viksjön is a lake in Sweden
Lime is used to neutralise acidic water

NEIL CURRY

Swallows and Tortoises

It was the Age of Reason.
And when spring broke in Selborne
And Timothy the tortoise did come forth

And march about, they had a feel
For his pulse, but could not find it;
Bawled at him through a speaking-trumpet
But he appeared not to regard it;

So they dunked him in a tub of water
To see if he could swim, and watched him
Go sinking down to scrabble on the bottom,
quite out of his element, and seemingly

Much dismayed. But what puzzled them most
In Selborne was that Providence
Should squander longevity
On a reptile who relished it so little

As to spend two-thirds of its existence
In a joyless stupor, all but the thread
Of solstitial awareness suspended.

But there were lessons to be learned everywhere,
And as Timothy awoke with the first flight
Of the swallows, might not they too
Have their *hybernacula*?

And had not Dr Johnson himself seen them
Conglobulate, before throwing themselves
Under water, wherein they would winter
On the bed of the river?

Sometimes Timothy escaped them,
Toddling his carapace out through the wicket:
Pursuits of an amorous kind transporting him
Beyond the bounds of his usual gravity.

FRED D'AGUIAR

The Cow *Perseverance*

I

Here I am writing you on old newspaper against a tide
    of print,
In the regular spaces between lines (there are no more
    trees).
I've turned it upside-down to widen the gap bordering
    sense and nonsense,
For what I must say might very well sound as if it were
    topsy-turvy.
I put myself in your shoes (unable to recall when I last
    set eyes on a pair).
You read everything twice, then to be doubly sure, aloud,
Testing their soundness: *we wash cow's dung for its grain,*
And I feel your stomach turn; it's not much unlike collect-
    ing it for fuel,
Or mixed with clay to daub cracks in our shelters and
    renew door-mounds
That free us of rain, insects and spirits. They no longer
    drop the milk
We let them live for; their nights spent indoors for safe
    keep,
Their days tethered to a nearby post. People eye them
    so, they are fast
Becoming our cross; you'd think they'd fallen out of the
    sky.

II

Hunger has filled them with what I can only call compassion.

Such bulbous, watery eyes blame us for the lack of grass and worse,

Expect us to do something; tails that held the edge of windscreen wipers

In better days, swishing the merest irritant, a feather's even,

Let flies congregate until the stretched, pock-marked hide is them.

That's why, when you asked how things were, I didn't have to look far,

I thought, *Let the cow explain, its leathery tongue has run this geography*

Many times over; how milk turns, unseen, all at once, so lush pastures

Threw up savannahs. The storms are pure dust or deep inside the rowdiest

Among us, virtually dead and rowdy because they know it, they're not sure

What else to do. You fathom why, when a cow croons we offer it

What we can't as a bribe for it to stop: *silence is perseverance*.

III

We watch its wait on meagre haunches, ruminating on
    what must be
Imperishable leather, some secret mantra, our dear
    buddha, for the miracle
We need; and us with nowhere to turn, find we believe.
    God knows
It's a case of choosing which pot-hole in the road to ride;
    knowing
We export the asphalt that could fill them; knowing too
    the one thing
We make these days that is expressly ours is whipped in
    malarial water
And forced down our throats for daring to open our
    mouths.
Give us the cow's complicity anyday: its perfect art of
    being left
In peace; its till-now effortless conversion of chewy grass
    to milk;
And its daft hoof-print, ignored for so long though clearly
    trespassing.
Then and then alone, we too can jump over the moon,
    without bloodshed.
Its raised-head and craned-neck attempt to furnish an
    exact account
Is a tale you and I are bound to finish, in flesh or spirit.

Penelope Rippon

HILARY DAVIES

Lemur

I came here first.
I had to myself the savannah
And the dark of the rain forest.
I ate the fruits at my ease
And picked the dew out of the flowers'
Cusp. I copulated
With my own kind, until each suited
Bush, or lolloping over
The ground, or watching everything
From the summit of the trees.
We grew fur all colours of the rainbow,
Hands more delicate than cobwebs,
Ears that could hear a grub
Crawling underground. Around us
Lifted the fortress of the immaculate sea.

I have grown cunning since then.
Our eyes perfected to see clearer
All things dark, the black
Moving at the heart of things.
We hide in the tree trunks at noonday,
Drop like stones out of the twilight.
My teeth have grown too large,
Show always through my lips like
A jaw decomposing. The new inhabitants
Fear my third digit: when I hear them
Coming like innocents through the undergrowth,
I crook my long finger to the one
I will favour, watch with my vast
And incurious eyes his companions
Lay out his incandescent white bones.

VINCENT DE SOUZA

Alive

The butchered reindeer is alive.
It rests on the ground,
The antlers are bloodstained
And the mouth is almost peaceful.
There are streaks of blood on the face,
It flows from the neck on to the wet mud,
And the pool is bright and fanciful,
There are brown swirls inside it,
Like you get in a child's painting.
The animal's eyes are open,
And I wonder how they worked . . .
Trap-doors to the next meal,
Cameras never quick enough,
I think of someone without imagination,
I think of the bits of beauty
That refuse to stick in my head.

CAROL ANN DUFFY

The Legend

Some say it was seven tons of meat in a thick black hide
you could build a boat from, stayed close to the river
on the flipside of the sun where the giant forests were.

Had shy, old eyes. You'd need both those hands for
one.
Maybe. Walked in placid herds under a jungly,
sweating roof
just breathing, a dry electric wind you could hear a mile
off.

Huge feet. Some say if it rained you could fish in a
footprint,
fruit fell when it passed. It moved, food happened,
simple.
You think of a warm, inky cave and you got its mouth
all right.

You dream up a yard of sandpaper, damp, you're
talking tongue.
Eat? Its own weight in a week. And water. Some say
the sweat steamed from its back in small grey clouds.

But *big*. Enormous. Spine like the mast on a galleon.
Happen. Ears like sails gasping for a wind. You
picture
a rope you could hang a man from, you're seeing its
tail.

Tusks like bannisters. I almost believe myself. Can you
drum up a roar as wide as a continent, a deep hot note
that bellowed out and belonged to the melting air? You
    got it.

But people have always lied! You know some say it had
    a trunk
like a soft telescope, that it looked up along it at the sky
and balanced a bright, gone star on the end, and it died,
    died.

HELEN DUNMORE

Not Going to the Forest

If you had said the words 'to the forest'
at once I would have gone there
leaving my garden of broccoli and potato plants,

I would not have struggled

to see the last ribbons of daylight
and windy sky tear over the crown
of the oaks which stand here,
heavy draught animals
bearing, continually bearing.

I would have rubbed the velvety forest
against my cheek like the pincushion
I sewed with invisible stitches.

No. But you said nothing
and I have a child to think of
and a garden of parsnips and raspberries.
It's not that I'm afraid
but that I'm still gathering
the echoes of my five senses -

how far they've come with me, how far
they want to go on,

so the whale-back of the forest
shows for an instant, then dives.
I think it has oxygen within it
to live, downward, for miles.

Robbie Burns

DOUGLAS DUNN

Hothouse February

No-one expects such snow
When the peach tree blooms
In its world of window.
White wind and wintry brooms –

They didn't last. Warm time
Returns, and daffodils,
In February, chime
Their northern April bells.

What shall you do, creatures,
Inhabiting my eyes?
This land is ours and yours,
Its rivers and its skies.

Hens feeding on their species
Should shame us out of sleep.
Instead, we court disease
And feed our cows on sheep.

Polluted verse can't make
Sense of the upside-down,
A hemisphere's mistake
Offensive to the sun.

Man-made industrial guilt
Means nothing to the birds
On threatened trees that lilt
To songs without words

By sea, Eden, or loch,
Superior to this –
A natural coronach
For life and wilderness.

NOTE: *The Eden is a river in Fife*

D. J. ENRIGHT

Conservation

You lift it cautiously on a pole
And you cast it over the wall
And into the neighbouring compound.
(You do not wish to kill,
You do not wish to be killed
Or suffer in other respects.)
In the neighbouring compound
Short cries ensue or vexed sighs,
Then they hook it carefully on a pole
And heave it over the wall
And into the adjacent garden.
(They do not wish to kill,
Or be killed or incommoded.)
Then in the adjacent garden
Someone will pick it up on a pole
(The kind that every householder keeps
Against these contingencies)
And sling it warily over the wall.

By the law of eternal recurrence,
That serpentine cycle,
One day it reaches your compound again
(You have had peace in the meantime)
And you lift it up on a pole –
Unless you perceive it has died of bruising
Or age or weakening of the will to live
And be tossed repeatedly over a wall,
In which case you simply ignore it
Or fork it into the garden –
If not, you pick up the snake on a pole
And you cast it cautiously. . . .

GAVIN EWART

Crying Wolf?

Is it a joke when the poets cry doom?
When Alan Brownjohn writes a poem about the Last
    Rabbit,
about the Ultimate Bunny?
And Larkin imagines all the green fields being concreted
    over?
Is it *funny*?

It may never happen – we all assume,
as the trees go into the popular large-circulation papers
and acid rains fall in a shower.
We still have the telly, polluted rivers, lots of blue
    politicians
and nuclear power. . .

So far: no world-ending atomic boom.
It's like Dr Who and the Cybermen and the Daleks,
when the Larva Guns come creeping. . .
we're so used to the warheads and the constant
    electronic
pin-prick bleeping . . .

Chemical warfare? Should *we* fret and fume?
All these things happen in quite far-away countries.
Imagine the ozone layer,
can we? The greenhouse effect? A joke that slays us?
Yes, it could be a slayer!

RUTH FAINLIGHT

Driving

Each species is allotted its number of heartbeats.
A mouse has the same life span as myself or a whale
but lives it more quickly, at a different tempo.

The fluttering heat of a heart or a forest.
How many leaves to a kilometre?
I want to be astonished, but it happens less often.

Such solid coils of steam and smoke extruded from
the tall cone-chimneys of a power station,
like chalky turds defying the laws of gravity.

Trees and cars and clouds blur in the speed. I have seen
almost enough for a whole life – endless renewal
and repetition. The planet belongs to the trees.

VICKI FEAVER

Eagle Owl

It sits in a yew's high branches,
the afternoon sun
warming its blazoned breast.

It has feasted on sparrow and pigeon.
It snoozes like a magistrate
after the morning session.

A small crowd gathers,
necks craned backwards
as if awaiting a judgment.

The rumour goes round –
a woman was swooped on
powdering her nose

as she crossed
the cathedral precinct at dusk –
it ought to be shot.

No-one knows where it comes from.
Escaped from a zoo,
one man suggests.

Someone else says
it's from the forests of Siberia
blown off-course in a storm.

For months its whooo-whooo
has echoed at nights
round buttress and boss.

I think it's Athena
come down to earth
this mild winter

to see if men
have grown any wiser:
elated at first

(she's not getting any younger)
to find she could still squeeze
into her feathery dress –

then suddenly feeling
too old, tired and discouraged
to make the long flight back.

'In the midst of a silktail flock'

Elizabeth Blackadder

JAMES FENTON

The Orange Dove of Fiji

To R. and B. O'H

On the slopes of Taveuni
The Barking Pigeons woof
But when I saw the Orange Dove
I nearly hit the roof

And would have surely had there been
A roof around to hit
But the roofs of Taveuni
Are down on the lower bit

While up there in the forest
The Silktails have survived
And they forage in the 'substage'
And you feel you have *arrived*

As an amateur ornithologist
In the midst of a Silktail flock
Until you hear behind you
A 'penetrating tock'

And you find six feet above your head
What you were looking for –
The Orange Dove of Fiji,
No less, no more.

The female of the Orange Dove
Is actually green.
The really orange *male* Orange Dove
Is the one you've seen.

It must have been dipped in Dayglo
Held by its bright green head.

The colour is preposterous.
You want to drop down dead.

It turns around upon its perch
Displaying all the bits
That are mentioned in Dick Watling's book
And the description fits.

Then it says: 'Tock. Okay, is that
Enough to convince you yet?
Because that, my friend, is all tock tock
That you are going to get.'

Oh, the Many-Coloured Fruit Dove
Is pretty enough to boot
And I'm afraid the Purple Swamphen
Looks queerer than a coot

Like a flagrant English bishop
Let loose among his flock
With brand new orange gaiters
(And *that*'s just the Swamphen cock.)

But the Orange Dove is something
Spectacular to see.
So I hope they don't fell another single
Taveuni tree.

NOTE: Watling, *Birds of Fiji, Tonga and Samoa*, Croom, Helm,
1982

38

JENNIE FONTANA

Lioness

he clenches me between his knees
with his untufted tail tucked
into the cat-suit that reflects knives
into the blind lights
offers meat on a stick to keep me in position

faces strain at the drum roll
criss-crossed by mesh
their eyes bulge like antelope
before the kill

he puts his hands to prise my jaw
I yawn
and his stiff acid-haired head
closes in
no breath

the 'antelope' clap as he disconnects
(I will not satisfy their fear)
but it is the two mountain bears
that suck honeyed milk from bottles
and lick his face
that get the loud applause night after night

he spits 'cub killer!' at my curled lip
as he bolts my cage
he wanted to suckle them too
but they were dead when I turned
bloody
sacked in the straw

their perfect forms
velvet on my tongue
by the scruff

sweet swallow
and gone

my milk like bone my
five pace and turn
whiskers worn on the bars
no room for one pace more

no tug on a nipple
my milk like bone
his smiling skull
no savanna
no zebra no
no
no pain

PETER FORBES

Convergent Evolution

This is my favoured mode:
hardly any clothes, natural interest;
I pad from lake to shore to book
and lap my brain with speculation.
Reading Dawkins on evolution,
I squint and see it happen here:
Primitive molecules in the shallows where
the ducks upend and smallfry leap –
late twentieth-century humans at ease on the earth.

And the shrubs have a glaucous bloom
like the grapes, while your skin goes harvest
brown and I'm reading how life brought forth
mammals in their various trades –
browsers, predators, tunnelling moles –
while thousands perch like us in the sun,
a few reading Dawkins, while DNA
keeps the human plan, the presses print
the next bestseller and the floppy disks
keep our files in code; we must always converge
on a spot like this, humans by a lake
with all the elements we started with
and all the ingredients we need to live.

Annie Ovendon

JOHN FULLER

Bog

Kneeling for marshfruit like spilled
Beads bedded in displaying moss
I notice a licked frog dragging
His drenched fatigues up and through
The barring spears and stalks of orange
Bog asphodel as if in terror
Of unknown purposes, as though
I were a weight of sky, a whole
Universe of beak and gullet,
And not, as I am, a mere slider
And stumbler like him, damp to the hips,
Reaching for tussocks, scrabbling for almost
Nothing: these little speckled fruits,
Chill marbles of a forgotten tourney,
Aching playthings of a lost garden
That has always been mostly water,
A place of utter loneliness,
Terrain of the asphodel and of the frog.

ELIZABETH GARRETT

Against the World's Going

It is more than the sun's going or the gold
Declivity of wheat that draws us down
Again to where the broken field
Bears a cicatrice of fencing,
And a stream
Busy beneath its ravelled covering
Burrows like a worm.

It is something more than the want
To stay the scene's dispersing,
Straddle the stream with the scant
Ligature of thought,
Or trace the barbed stitching
With the infinite caution
Of a stranger's hand.

What is it homes me here
Like the unseen pulse of radar?
Elms along the skyline stick
Their wreckage; the air stirs
With the ceaseless swell of heat.
Nothing but brimming wheat
Remains unbroken.

Somewhere in space a pointer
Flickers and stops; I scan.
Silence; the suffocation before waking,
Till, like a dream, driftwood breaks
The surface of the corn,
A young stag rears his antlers,
Stark, against the world's going.

Silence; a drowned dusk;
This dwindling earth a pebble
Rolled and rubbed
Beneath heat, like waves,
Or hands on a grain of wheat,
A crumbling husk,
Inexorably rubbing.

Coelacanth

Après le déluge, moi. . .

Survivor of survivors
(was the Rock of Ages cleft for *this*?)

he's found his niche,
his deep-sea bunker,

his last ditch.
See the set of his jaw,

Churchillian . . .
Evolution

blunders overhead;
the wreckage comes sifting down.

He paces barren sea-slopes
on stiff fin-struts,

almost legs.
He'll get it right next time.

Meanwhile
there's the dark and the cold

and the tons per square inch
to hold him

tight.
On the face of the waters

there's a flirt and glance
and shudder to and fro

of life, like fans of wind.

46

TONY HARRISON

Art & Extinction

'When I hear of the destruction of a species I feel as if
all the works of some great writer had perished.'
(Theodore Roosevelt, 1899)

The Birds of America

(i) John James Audubon (1785–1851)

The struggle to preserve once spoken words
from already too well-stuffed taxonomies
is a bit like Audubon's when painting birds,
whose method an admirer said was this:
Kill 'em, wire 'em, paint 'em, kill a fresh 'un!

The plumage even of the brightest faded.
The artist had to shoot in quick succession
till all the feathers were correctly shaded.

Birds don't pose for pictures when alive!
Audubon's idea of restraint,
doing the Pelican, was 25
dead specimens a day for *one* in paint.

By using them do we save words or not?

As much as Audubon's art could save a,
say, godwit, or a grackle, which he shot
and then saw 'multiplied by Havell's graver'.

(ii) Weeki Wachee

Duds doomed to join the dodo: the dugong,
talonless eagles, croc, gimp manatee,
here, courtesy Creation's generous strong,
the losers of thinned jungle and slicked sea.

Many's the proud chieftain used to strut
round shady clearings of dark festooned teak
with twenty cockatoo tails on his nut,
macaw plumes à la mode, rainforest chic.

Such gladrag gaudies safe in quarantine
and spared at least their former jungle fate
of being blowpiped for vain primitives to preen
now race a tightrope on one roller skate.

A tanned sophomore, these ghettoed birds' Svengali,
shows glad teeth, evolved for smiling, as macaws
perform their deft Darwinian finale
by hoisting the Stars and Stripes for our applause.

(iii) Standards

in hopeful anticipation of the bicentenary of the national
emblem of the United States of America, *Haliaaetus Falco
Leucocephalus*, 1782–1982

'The bald eagle is likewise a large, strong, and very
active bird, but an execrable tyrant: he supports his
assumed dignity and grandeur by rapine and violence,
extorting unreasonable tribute and subsidy from the
feathered nations.' (William Bartram, *Travels*, 1791)

'Our standard with the eagle stands for us.
It waves in the breeze in almost every clime.'

(The flag, not *Falco Leucocephalus*
poised in its dying on the brink of time!)

Rejecting Franklin's turkey for a bird that *flies*
Congress chose the soaring eagle, called,
for its conspicuous white head, 'the bald'.
Now the turkey's thriving and the eagle dies!

When the last stinks in its eyrie, or falls slow,
when the very last bald eagle goes the way
of all the unique fauna, it won't know
the Earth it plummets to 's the USA.

But will still wing over nations as the ghost
on money, and the mountainous US Post

much as sunlight shining through the British pound
showed PEACE with her laurels, white on a green
   ground.

FRANCIS HARVEY

Heron

was assembled out of bits and scraps, not made.
Like one of those early flying machines held together
   with glue and twine.
His undercarriage is an afterthought sticking out
   behind.
He is all wings and no fuselage and probably hollow
   inside.
Finn could have blown him off the palm of his hand.

He creaks into flight. The wind buffets him, gives him
a bumpy ride: it seems he must somehow end up
in a twisted heap of canvas and struts on the
   mountainside.
But no: he tacks into weathers with a prow that rises
   and falls in the swell.
The ghost of the pterodactyl haunts him in every cell.

He alights: furls his wings like a wet umbrella, settles,
   rapt and murderous,
drying out in the wind and sun on the edge of a tarn
or hunched over a pool in the burn pretending he's
a blind one-legged beggarman or a mystic communing
   with God.
Too late, too late for the fish or frog when it realises
   he's not an old cod!

Heron invented slow motion long before the movies
   came but
allows himself the lightning of his pickaxe for the killing
   game.
Heron's the icon of the silences beyond the last tongues
of land where the islands float and quiver like mirages
   in the light,

he's the hermit who daily petrifies himself in the reeds
    of the penitential lake,

the logo of the lonely places past the last sheep and the
    last house,
the El Greco or Modigliani doodle in a remote corner of
    the evening sky where
the newsprint of distant waders swims before the eye,
Heron's that sudden outlandish screech you hear at
    midnight
in the water meadows as he changes into the wrong
    gear.

Roger de Gray

SEAMUS HEANEY

The Road at Frosses

Not an avenue and not a bower.
For a quarter-mile or so, where the county road
Is running straight across North Antrim bog,

Tall old fir trees line it on both sides.
Scotch firs, that is. Calligraphic shocks
Bushed and tufted in prevailing winds.

You drive into a meaning made of trees.
Or not exactly trees. It is a sense
Of running through and under without let,

Of glimpse and dapple. A life all trace and skim
The car has vanished out of. A fanned nape
Sensitive to the millionth of a flicker.

SELIMA HILL

Dorothy

Not only daggers, hatchets and lobelia
gleam like butter in the hot interior,

but here, not stopping, busy as a bee –
half a sort of tapir, half a flea –

a yellow shrew is jumping up and down
on tiny toes that titillate the ground,

and pepper its vermilion shifting sands
with ancient secrets no-one understands:

everything's alright, she seems to say,
as long as I am free to go my way –

hopping in and out of red tomatoes,
copper grasses, elegant flamingoes,

chasing ants – and hiding from zoologists,
who'll carry me away, and call me 'Dorothy',

and tell me quietly not to be alarmed.
I'll be inspected, tidied up and calmed:

calm as shells or peaches in a bowl;
or chapel windows overlooking snow;

the smell of myrrh; the luxury of silk;
lupins in the garden; sweetened milk.

Pray for guidance to the god of shrews –
he will know which is the life to choose!

A Cup of Kindness

Reindeer calve; the dotterel
sings in the sedge like tin;

small Lapps net chard, and white milk
mixed with sorrel sours in kegs;

a baby, sucking bones in a willow-bush
is dreaming in a world of fur and cloud;

while, overhead, two patient botanists
try and remember the words of Auld Lang Syne.

MICHAEL HOFMANN

Pastorale

for Beat Sterchi

Where the cars razored past on the blue highway,
I walked, unreasonably, *contre-sens*,

the slewed census-taker on the green verge,
noting a hedgehog's defensive needle-spill,

the bullet-copper and bullet-steel of pheasants,
henna ferns and a six-pack of *Feminax*,

indecipherable cans and the cursive snout and tail
of a flattened rat under the floribund ivy,

the farmer's stockpiled hayrolls and his flocks,
ancillary, bacillary blocks of anthrax.

TED HUGHES

What the Serpent Said to Adam

If the sky is infected
The river has to drink it

If earth has a disease that could be fatal
The river has to drink it

If you have infected the sky and the earth
Caught its disease off you – you are the virus

If the sea drinks the river
And the earth drinks the sea

It is one quenching and one termination

If your blood is trying to clean itself
In the filter of your flesh
And the sores run – that is the rivers

The five rivers of Paradise

Where will you find a pure drink now?

Already, look, the drop has returned to the cup

Already you are your ditch, and there you drink

ROBERT INGHAM

Sellafield from St Bees Head

The wind blew your words away
On the cliff walk,
Even the sea that day
Could not talk;
The smoke to the south was grey.

Your words were snatched and hurled
With other trifles, scraps
Of the daily world,
Carried perhaps
To the dead; the smoke unfurled.

The dead wait at the wind's end,
Lipless, to suck
What little we send,
They have no luck,
They are dead; we began to descend.

We walked on the beach and saw
Where the sea's long tongue
Had licked the pebbles raw
And the little shells that clung
Like scabs along the jaw.

I heard the sea's voice break
With some impediment,
It was not able to make
Me understand what it meant;
The wind made our bones ache.

PETER JAY

The Third Planet

There were creatures on the third
planet from that small star.
We knew from their signals that
the two-legged upright mammals
possessed intelligence: how
did they come to perish? And with them
thousands of species: fish and fowl,
mammal, insect, reptile?
Their only song now is the song of the wind.

Their remains are beneath the sands:
traces of vegetation, rich
fossil-hoards, mass graveyards –
monuments to their estrangement
from the planet they called 'earth'.
an electrical metaphor signifying
the attunement to their surroundings
which their poets praised.
Their only song now is the song of the wind.

Cancer on cancer killed them.
They were adept in poisons:
did they strip their sclerotic planet
of its atmospheric protection,
letting the sun pour down
in all its merciless candour,
the sun that gave them life
taking all life-forms away?
Their only song now is the song of the wind.

This was our fabled south Pole Star:
its inhabitants great and small
are bones under the deserts,
in dried sea-beds and swamps,
their once-proud earthen riches
crumbled to global dust.
What is a world without bird-song?
Sundry lichens survive.
Their only song now is the song of the wind.

anonymous Arcturan poet, c. 40,000 AD
translated by Peter Jay

ALAN JENKINS

Log

'The maelstrom! Could a more dreadful word in a more
dreadful situation have sounded in our ears! . . . From every
point of the horizon enormous waves were meeting, forming
a gulf justly called 'The Navel of the Ocean', whose power
of attraction extends to a distance of twelve miles. There, not
only vessels, but whales are sacrificed, as well as white bears
from the northern regions.'
                    – Jules Verne, *Twenty Thousand Leagues Under the Sea*

Myself, Fairford and the boy, deck-hands on the *Scarface*
(A.G. Pym, Tokyo-Nantucket) were huddled by Buxton,
  who took the wheel,
and Captain George Currie – when Jenkins, gnawing a
  frostbitten sole
turns to us his fat white moustache of frost and ice,
fluffy-looking, like a kid all stuck with candy-floss
or ice-cream from a cornet – but with something of his
  Dad's,
who was in whalers before him (*his* Dad remembered
  the days of sail).
At first he'd laughed, called it *the rime of the ancient*
mariners,
but now he turned with a glint in his eye, shouted
  Steady lads!
This here's the maelstrom, the navel of the ocean!
- sort of barmy voice. We thought he'd begun to rave
but looked out, scraping white stars from the ports of
  the deckhouse
and saw, miles around, from every point of the horizon,
running towards the gulf, enormous wave on wave . . .

It was weeks since we'd lost sight of the fleet – seen
  only pack-ice
drifting farther and farther south, and not a single
  whale,
not a single living thing, neither sea-bird nor seal;
then yesterday, early morning watch, Soutar cried out
  twice -
Fuckin' Christ man there's bears on it, and peering under
  the fleece
of our hoods we could see them moving, outlines,
  shadows,
white on whiter white; and terror stabbed each soul
at how long we'd been steaming north. We stood like
  mourners
as Cladd ran for'ard, fired; watched the spirit that was
  Cladd's
explode out of him in a white cloud, a frosty exhalation.
Chedglow chipped him off of the gun with an ice-pick;
we boiled and ate most of him, stewed with scurvy-
  cress,
stowed the leftovers, the dainties, in the empty freezer.
Last night I dreamt of dressed fingers, toes in aspic,

and today we saw the bear we'd skewered – one more
  sacrifice,
crumpled, wasted . . . A moment later we hit the swell,
white swirls, foam plunging, *each wave swallowin' itsel'*
Soutar screamed, and we were drawn in, down, but
  not to a green-white peace -
for there alongside us, as we sank further from the
  floes,
swam a multitude of dead or dying things: otters, gulls,
  their eyelids
clogged shut, fur and feathers claggy with effluents, oil;
among the whaling-boats, trawlers, ketches, catamarans
we saw blood-spattered seals; tunny trailing swim-
  bladders;
whales spilling pink froth, each stuck like a huge pincushion

with harpoons; pocked, distended creatures, as from a
    blasted Ark -
all this Jenkins begged me to set down, not to secure
    for us
pardon, still less Larsen's fame, but to be our only
    blazon
should we come back alive out of this deep cold, this
    dark.

ROY KELLY

Snail Nation

The snail, that inhabitant of damp corners,
friend of children, is the pest of gardeners.
It is hermaphrodite, and can copulate
simultaneously with both sexes. It
is also a cupid, for to stimulate
its prospective mate it will shoot at it a
tiny, four-fluted, crystalline dart which it
keeps in a quiver next to the glands on its
female duct. The maximum range of its shot

is two and a half inches. It has other
curious habits. Its eyes are on the ends
of its horns, and when it has indigestion
it can put one of them down its gullet to
see what the trouble is. When it has to cross
a rough patch of ground it lays down a carpet
of slime from a foot gland to make the passage
smoother. Every child should keep a snail farm
of many species, and make them run races.

* * *

No part of the world they do not inhabit.
The deepest ocean trench when dredged
produces specimens. Lakes of ice and sky
on Himalayan peaks, close as the eye of God,
secrete them in their lonely tenacity.
Gastropoda, of the phylum Mollusca,
the belly-footed ones who glide the planet
in numbers beyond imagining, beyond the mind
which can picture mountain peaks and ocean depths.

Fifty thousand species. Fifty thousand specific types.
And how many million individuals?
Inconspicuous and abundant beyond the mind's
    imagining.

How many atoms dance in the eye of God?
Marine and brackish-water and freshwater and land
belly-footed ones gliding God's golf ball.
Snowbanks in Alpine meadows, deserts in Egypt,
know Gastropoda of the phylum Mollusca.
Old as time, slugs orange as fruit, snails be-jewelled
    with calcareous whorls.

Prosobranchs, opistobranchs, and pulmonates
showing a great variety of structure
are excellent to demonstrate evolutionary principle,
being as old as the world, primitive and sophisticated
as Himalayan snow meadows, Egyptian deserts, ocean
    deeps.
Periwinkles. Queen conches. Abalone. Turban snails.
Ornamented with shells of Japanese artistry
Gastropoda of the phylum Mollusca
with many names. Scavengers and delicacies.
Desert snails have lived without food and water
in museum collections for six years.
Under natural conditions they could perhaps go longer.
And what conditions are natural, and how shall we
    keep them so?
And who will fund the museum under God's eye
containing fifty thousand separate species
going about secretive, abundant, useful work,
millions to the square mile, sheathed in shell and slime,
digesting the products of death and decay.

                    *   *   *

Death and decay and poisoning through ignorance
as world nations, nations of God's golf ball, our lonely,
    only planet,
creep inconspicuously to inadequate legislation.
Snail-like, sluggish, the nations crawl unwilling to their
    diet of words,
under skies dark with delay, dubious with
    apprehension.
A chlorofluorocarbon magnifying glass is forcing

65

the issue, sheeting the atmosphere, transforming
a living museum into a greenhouse burning to please.
Sleeved in chemical air, polluted unprivate oceans warm
to their task. Polar caps melt into the night.

The acid rain of embittered propaganda
splashes out with stair rod rhetoric,
the drizzle of deception, posturing, bombast,
explaining how money is at the root of everything.
You cannot throw money at problems and expect magic
they say. You think problems will disappear? They say.
But what is money except fossilised magic?
Add it to water. Retire. It causes appearance,
      disappearance.
Holes are magicked in ozone, clouds in stratosphere.
Money can do anything but understand what it is doing.

Fleeced and clouded the future floats in space,
and God must bank on nations economical with truth
      and economy.
Primitive and sophisticated demonstrations of evolution
we operate on erratic principle, fear and self-interest
predominating. We come to carbon burning, burning.
A fossil fuel cannibalises fossil fuel in a parody,
a litany of sins committed and omitted,
a chemical romance contaminated with convenience.
And now amongst others lead, mercury, aluminium,
      cadmium, zinc,
in addition to iron must penetrate the soul.

                    *   *   *

As of bone china,
or eggshell, a thin crackle
on the midnight path.

An innocent shoe
has come to the crunch. Careless.
Unknowing but stained

with consequences.
Something dies slowly in slime,
in fragments and slime.

* * *

And Gastropoda of the phylum Mollusca
populate the planet, digesting death and decay.
But not shoes. But not salt. But not poison.
Oozing into the slime that cannot wash them free,
and cannot wash us free, and cannot wash us free.

* * *

Money and truth sleeved in chemical air
the future floats, hanging in space,
redeemable, hanging there.

* * *

An empty shell's an earring for a corpse.

Acknowledgements to *Encyclopaedia Britannica* and Gerald Brenan's
Thoughts in a dry season from which some of the poem's text has been
adapted.

Sue Cave

JOHN LEVETT

The Butterfly Centre

for Ruth

Too pretty by half their chalks and flicked inks
Lift-off from gravel and circle the plants,
Up to their bright, barometric high-jinks,
Dodging down drinkable flightpaths of chance
To customize sunshine, flicker and lurch,
Vamp and soft-pedal, cant over and skim;
Taut, narcissistic, outspread to research
Each dickering paint-chart's unfixable whim:

Tranquilized lilacs, regressions of gold,
Haunted manillas and shoaled, nitrous blues,
Skeletal lemons, quick lacings of mould
Swallowtails sew by your black canvas shoes.
Their hand-woven gimmicks tickle the air
Grazing from pad to ephemeral pad
And leapfrogging ferns that scaffold the glare
To touch down on netting's trembled brocade.

Distracted you turn and crane over the pond
Where gnats refuel above urinous rocks
And crapulous goldfish decay with their blond
Submarine passions, your dazzled white socks
Stepping from childhood and onto a brink,
Steadied for something more solid and real
Than promises lit by these papery winks
Or the heat that inherits their vanished appeal.

GEORGE MACBETH

Remembering the Bad Things

For instance, every time he drove down that road
In the dark, or even during the day, in sunlight,
He remembered the small grey streak from the
   hedgerow

And then the slight impact, nothing very significant
In a big car, and wondering for several seconds
What it was he had struck, maybe the sheepdog

That was always rushing out under his wheels,
Crouching and then attacking, as if he was a stranger
And not the familiar large shape that rolled by every day.

But no, it was no dog. He remembered stopping
The car a hundred yards on, and reversing back
To where the once-living rag lay in the road.

He remembered opening the door, and walking forward
In the blaze of his headlamps, full beam in the dark
On the sprawl of a long cat, a toothpaste of blood

Oozing out of its mouth, and the eyes wide
On the far side of the road it would never reach.
O yes, he remembered the tears coming, useless tears

For not being careful enough, and then he remembered
Lifting the little corpse in his arms, warm and limp.
And laying it aside to rest for ever in the grass.

There were other bad things, but this was one
He always remembered, knowing his own three cats
Alive and safe in the house, not half a mile away.

And someone crying, like him, for the loss of a dear
    one.

Ann Arnold

EVE MACHIN

Wiltshire Autumn

This is our season
when the downs, harrowed for winter
hold their seeds of wheat and barley
and on waves surging into distant mist
curved and frilled fossils
of cretaceous sea.

Perennial lapwings
hop and flutter
against mild pebble-mottled slopes,
call, merge and are silent.

In water-meadows
the russet sorrel droops,
puffballs drift in the cooling air,
sap is sinking.

This is our season
holding a tilted land in quiet,
with below, the river running.

LACHLAN MACKINNON

The Dream of Gallifrey

Tamarisk feathers,
high sunset cloud,
sunset the usual
eight minutes late.
The next star
is more than four years back.

Our eyes adjust.
Space crawls with stars and curves
to cup them like the red
plastic solitaire board
my brothers knelt at.
Their light drags, red.

Everything falls away
from our horizon,
backward and out,
only machines
near the dim heat,
the howl

of the beginning
everything flies from
like shaky deer
out of a flaming forest,
the moment vacuum
wobbled and burst.

The pretty constellations
are strung out
like a perspective exercise
and move as we move,
too slowly
to change our quick behaviour.

When my parents
installed their first fridge,
did they reckon
they were wrecking the planet?
Well, we blame them
as surely as the stars,

unwilling to concede
time points to us to find for what
wedding, what funeral,
earth trails the heavens like a veil.
I was a boy
when men walked

on the face of the huntress.
Gently bending incoming light
she rises, less
than a minute behind us,
earth's ashen, ruined sister
no doctor heals.

E. A. MARKHAM

Long Lines from the Island

He was of a certain age, the dad, convicted with due
  cause to his room.
(Unlike an animal tied somewhere and fretting, he was
  contented with his lot.)
She was in another world where hopes which flew high
  as aeroplanes were not supposed to crash –
though she knew better, Mimijune, Julieblossom, with
  brothers to protect her, and a green skirt trailing like
  a target.
On the island he stopped and started disciplines,
  families, shopped around like a spendthrift seeking
  value.
And she was giddy in the air, on the ground, trailing
  her green skirt like a banner.

He was the old house, the island, hanging learning up
  to dry like Nellie's sheets free of salt;
hanging facts and logic on any old dog or cat, draping
  philosophies on the passing stranger
(rewriting the history of the world, renaming the
  children, the presidents and the gods).
She was separated from partners, each fighting his
  battle: the tripping up in London, the slight in Rome,
  stale bagels in New York.
She was there, where a telephone to report the crash
  didn't work: it was here.
And she is found staggering from a National Park in
  the cause of elephant and rhino.

There were those who saw her, green skirt above her
  head like the heroine of an Australian film stopping
  the traffic;
the same skirt trapped in the door of the car, cruising

76

(and her brothers, the Generals and Marshalls
reverting to type).
Then she was a silver train serving passengers as they
wished; some who saw the mistake
and were patient, read by her light as they entered the
tunnel which echoed:
why are the faces of animals expressionless as riddles?
where is there fresh government of bagels?
And back on the island she would confront an inmate
who still refused to be bought off with god knows
what degrees and victories.

GERDA MAYER

The Inheritor

I the sophisticated primate
Have stunted fingers on my feet,
And almost I control my climate,
And Everything is what I eat.

I wrote the story of Creation
when I discovered nudity:
The world is yours for exploitation.
I gave this charter unto me.

I traded in for my survival
My peaceful heart, my flealined coat;
Outpaced my vegetarian rival.
I have Creation by the throat.

JAMIE McKENDRICK

Ill Wind

To talk of the weather was a morbid sign.
The winds blew wherever they wanted to
raining their freight of dust.
A week before, the Sirocco had come
with its tiny pouches of sand, transplanting
one grain at a time, the whole Sahara;
silting the windows with a fine tan.
But this was a wind from the north that blew
across frontiers, ignoring the customs.
If it blew somewhere else the papers were glad.

I brushed a spider from the web it'd spun
between my arm and what seemed to be air -
it fell by a thread then hobbled off,
its fifth or its sixth leg giving it trouble.
'Will they survive it all' you asked 'the insects?'
I remembered the mutation-rates we'd studied
of the fruit fly (short-, long- and cross-winged)
and a luminous dream I'd had of origin:
life spiralling out from the cradled cell
through the basking oceanic forms.

And though the leaves were still I heard the wind
snicking the links with its casual shears.

STUART MILSOM

Sparrows and Others, Mid-April

Magpies follow one another
through the spare hedgerows
leaving impressions of a spread wing,
a frayed curve,
and the energy of their coupling.

The industry goes on, sparrows at their stonework,
feeding on invisible lichen
or preening in pools.

Under a seagull's shadow they go,
seeming no more of bone
than would sew up their feathers.

As crows take up twigs
with a dark, muscular flap
forbidding their naked homes

and trees slowly clothe like creatures
in their own weight and essence.

Never were the songs so sharp,
never were they so in evidence.

BLAKE MORRISON

On Sizewell Beach

There are four beach huts, numbered 13 to 16,
each with net curtains and a lock.
Who owns them, what happened to the first twelve,
whether there are plans for further building:
there's no one here today to help with such enquiries,
the café closed up for the winter,
no cars or buses in the PAY AND DISPLAY.
The offshore rig is like a titan's diving board.
I've heard the rumours that it's warmer here
for bathing than at any other point along the coast.
Who started them? The same joker who bought
the village pub and named it the Vulcan,
'God of fire and metalwork and hammers,
deformed and buffoonish, a forger of rich thrones'?
Whoever he is, whatever he was up to,
he'd be doused today, like these men out back,
shooting at clay pigeons, the rain in their Adnams beer.
And now a movement on the shingle
that's more than the scissoring of terns:
a fishing boat's landed, three men in yellow waders
guiding it shorewards over metal-ribbed slats
which they lay in front of it like offerings
while the winch in its hut, tense and oily,
hauls at the hook in the prow, the smack with its catch
itself become a catch, though when I lift
the children up to see the lockjaws of sole and whiting
there's nothing in there but oilskin and rope.

I love this place, its going on with life
in the shadow of the slab behind it,
which you almost forget, or might take for a giant's
    Lego set,
so neat are the pipes and the chain-mail fences,
the dinky railway track running off to Leiston,

the pylons like a line of cross-country skiers,
the cooling ponds and turbine halls and reactor control
   rooms
where they prove with geigers on Open Days
('Adults and Children over 14 years only')
that sealed plutonium is less radioactive than a watch.

One rain-glossed Saturday in April
a lad from Halesworth having passed his test
and wanting to impress his girlfriend
came here in the Ford he'd borrowed from his father
and took the corner much too fast, too green to judge
the danger or simply not seeing the child
left on the pavement by the father – no less reckless -
who had crossed back to his Renault for the notebook
he'd stupidly forgotten, the one with jottings
for a poem about nuclear catastrophe,
a poem later abandoned, in place of which
he'd write of the shock of turning round
to find a car had come between him and his daughter,
an eternity of bodywork blotting out the view,
a cloud or an eclipse which hangs before the eyes
and darkens all behind them, clearing at last
to the joy of finding her still standing there,
the three of us spared that other life we dream of
where the worst has already happened
and we are made to dwell forever on its shore.

ANDREW MOTION

The Great Globe

The border was neither wide nor deep, but it took a
    day
to sieve it, working through sprays of gravel, London
    clay,
and the bonfire-wrecks left by people before us:
sheets of sick iron, charred bottles, batteries leaking
    pus.

I thought of Joanna: the brittle white china body
I smashed, she smashed and hid, but which still stabs
    up at me
out of the deep solid earth wrestling and fretting like
    the sea.

PETER NORMAN

Sea Bird Watching

i
Divers

The bird guide works on Darwinian lines,
culminating with the *passeriformes*:
complex, acrobatic songsters.

At the front, on the lowest rung,
primitive loons that fly hump-backed.
in grey, stocking-mask hoods.

On land they're vulnerable, belly-flopping
to rudimentary nests, filling
the northern night with inchoate moans.

But when they surface on the tarn,
long, dark, cigar-shaped dreadnaughts,
they strike fear at the base of the brain.

ii
Fulmars

The tube-noses are a romantic order:
shearwaters, Mother Carey's Chickens
flitting the Atlantic swell like bats,
and Baudelaire's stricken monarch,
the star-crossed, wandering albatross.

But these marbled imposters,
unsuitable to sublime northern crags,
have colonized our domestic coasts
posing as plump, sad-eyed gulls
with heavy double-barrelled bills.

From clifftop turf you look down
at their incessant, solitary coming
and going, sweeping up and out again
on canted, impossibly stiff wings,
and learn the meaning of patience.

iii
Gannets

are all Persil-white wingspan
below a gun-metal horizon,
rising and plunging noiselessly
like sleek, state-of-the-art gulls.

But at close quarters, on Bass Rock,
where they snow down in thick drifts
to raise in gobbling intimacy
their fluff-brown, saurian offspring,

you can see their piss-stained necks
and alien, Dan-Dare masks:
compelling evidence
of evolution's warped talent.

SEAN O'BRIEN

Thirteen and Counting

A Guides' enrolment ceremony was held on the pile cap of Bradwell Nuclear Power Station in Essex on 18 January 1989. The girls wore no protective clothing except hard-hats. Neither their Guide Captain, their parents, nor the girls were informed that three leaks had occurred, in September and October 1988 and on 4 January 1989. The girls, all between ten and thirteen, belong by reason of their age and sex to the group most vulnerable to the effects of low level radiation.

Nothing political happens to them,
The thirteen girls who ascended the pile.

Up in Essex they care for their animals,
Honour the Queen and look forward to camp,

To the flags of the nations, the singing,
Night walks in the woods, the First Aid

With a strong cup of tea. In the albums
Are photos the families mean to raise laughter

In children of children, of girls on the pile
In their hard-hats, excited and formal

And raising their hands to enrol.
There is nothing to see but their pleasure.

Their hair and their shoes are not burning.
The weather was cold but the day a success

And they passed through the screens without ticking,
So that was a memory, perfect.

Three days when it leaked were quite different:
You just have to look at the dates.

So they didn't need suits or shoes even.
Their Captain, their parents, had no need to know,

And still less the thirteen, of the troublesome spot
Which occurred on the pile cap floor.

What it is to be young, in the Guides,
Before politics, thirteen and counting.

BERNARD O'DONOGHUE

Lepidus Timidus Hibernicus

Familiar of ditches, coming and going
Over the headland in the boggy acre
Where his form is. A bird of ill omen,
The old woman said, blessing herself.
There he goes (if you have the misfortune
To see him), pulsing away, tan brown
As the wary wren on the polish tin.

'I bless myself because, if he is shot
In the leg, they say I, here in my kitchen
Coven, will find my shoe filling with blood
While I comb out increasingly white tresses.'

Which is maybe why it's with our blessing that
Greyhounds slaver in their slipstream to savage
These initiates that spring vibrant from the last
Golden sheaf: such awesome cabbage-stags
Or furze-cats as preside in their hundreds
At Aldergrove, while the jet's whine rises
To hysteria, before taking soldiers
Or civilians towards death or joy or injury.

FIONA PITT-KETHLEY

Bird Watching

Bad men, it's said, behave 'like animals'.
(If beasts should ever imitate mankind
we'd never call our lives our own again.)

Next life, I'm going up the social scale.
Four feet? Too risky! Men might have my hide.
A bird? No chicken though – they're factory-farmed.
I'll settle for a gull's life by the sea.

My first few years, a dopey speckled thing
with sloe-black eyes and long St Trinian's legs
like wrinkled stockings with brown leather feet,
I start by picking mussels from the beach
and bathe in boating lakes among my kind.
Then, growing bolder, I will leave my home
to fly from coast to coast, try city life
and feast on junk, join ferries bound for France
or ride the thermals high above the cliffs.

At five, with all my childhood freckles gone,
demure in white and grey, I seek a mate –
bigger and stronger, but much like myself,
with kind, straw-coloured eyes as mild as mine,
an orange beak and long thin, clapper-tongue,
a deep pink throat that opens roaring wide
for bleakly-operatic Cockney cries.

I keep my head down when I see the gull
I want (males like that act). Convinced I'm not
a threat, he lets me move into his pad.

In Spring, I lead him on with cooing cries.
He says sex feels like flying on my back.

He takes his turn upon our clutch of eggs
and feeds me while I'm housebound – that's his job.
We kick the heads of humans who come near.
I test this mate of mine – if he protects
our mutual investment, then I'm his
for life. Divorce looms otherwise . . .

Our marriage, made in heaven, seems to last –
no money problems, mortgage, DIY –
the roof we share never cost *us* a cent.
Our nest's a mess, but we don't care a toss.
We're out a lot, you see. Our kids are fine –
a little stupid, true – but they will learn.
Our sons can fly at least – well, just about.
It's time they left. It's time we were alone.

This incarnation round I feed four gulls.
They breakfast shortly after dawn each day.
The males knock on my window with their beaks.
While I look out at them, the birds look in.

Next time, when I become a herring-gull,
I hope to keep some data in my head . . .
Charm humans and make friends of them.
Councillors order culls, believing gulls
will multiply by two by two by two:
endear yourself to those who'll make a fuss
about the 'sacredness of life' and tell
those nincompoops no creature breeds to form
and there are casualties from storms and oil.
Charm humans, but don't get too close to them . . .
Keep off their runways and their aeroplanes,
don't tread on glass, be careful of their tips,
eschew the plastic from their packs of beer
and never catch their tit-bits in your beak –
just let them drop – then look before you eat.

PETER PORTER

Frogs Outside Barbischio

How reassuring to listen to frogs once more
From stagnant water in an old brick cistern
Beside olive trees run wild and the unprogrammed
Flight of a butterfly over hot fields and terraces.
One grandfather frog stays on his stick to watch
This self-tormenter return to his book to trace
His anatomy of melancholy. He's in Italy
To surprise an old hopelessness known long before.

The cosmos of frogs inside its wet-walled fort
Warbles and cavorts in the all that there is.
Wise frog rejoinders have challenged that book:
Come down to our waters so pulsingly black
And lose all your stubble of fortune and truth.
Here's art inside art, incision and sign
Of the purposeless minute outlasting its span,
Of the gloat and the plop and the stick still afloat.

SIMON RAE

Keep the Rain Forest Burning

The destruction of the Amazonian rain forest (largely for short term profit from ranching and mining) is contributing to the 'greenhouse effect'. It is estimated that an area the size of Belgium was destroyed last year.

'Gallant little Belgium'
Used to be enough
To mobilize the nation;
We even cut up rough
Over empty acres
Of rocks and sheep and stuff.

We've lent the sort of money
A major war would take,
Investing in what's clearly
A terrible mistake.
(Bankers looking sheepish,
But then they all eat steak.)

Now the great trees tumble,
A way of life's destroyed.
Cattle range the forest,
Dams make valleys void.
– Simply your free market,
We've millions unemployed.

Gallant Chico Mendes
Spoke for the oppressed:
Poverty's the problem;
Seeing *that's* the test.
He got forty bullets
Stapled through his chest.

Hunky double burgers
Plotting in the fridge;
Jungle burning nicely
Ridge by verdant ridge;
(Porsches floating sleekly
Over London Bridge).

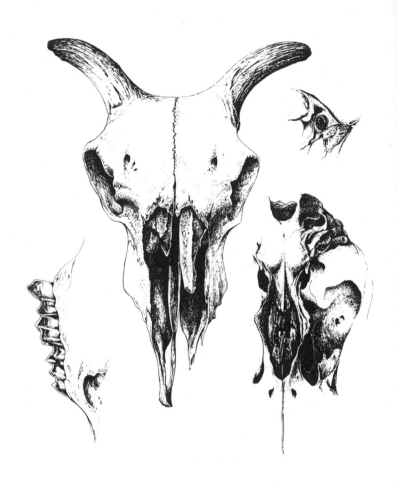

Brian Partridge

CRAIG RAINE

The Ram

A grey skull resting in the stream
on two symmetrical bone ringlets . . .

Trout nudge and glide
like flies under a bulb, oblivious

to the slow writhes of yellow horns.
I fetch it up, dripping,

and examine the cavities –
a cache of manuscripts, the sinuses

are scrolled like fine parchment;
egg-cup eyes; cracked china teeth . . .

The lower jaw is missing
and everything else besides,

scattered like Lycidas:
the chest and heavy genitalia

of a ram caked in his fleece
like a mud-pack,

clipping down the moorland road
regular as a clock . . .

Here are the broken mainsprings
and the grin that shed a body.

PETER READING

Ye haue heard this yarn afore

(but I'm minded on it againe
thefe daies of fqualls and rank clouds
and raines as is uitriolic –
pines fhorn ftark as mizzen-mafts
wi neuer a frolicfome fowl –
and ye top-gallant air all rent):

how we was one Monday anchored
off Mafcarenhas Iflande
in fourteen fathom o water;
how, feeking diuerfion, we landed;
how, on ye trees, there was pigeons
as blue as polifhed flate
which fuffered vs, being fo tame,
for to pluck em iuft like fruits
from ye branches and pull their necks;
how we killed two hundred firft day;
how we alfo killed grey paraquets
(moft entertayninge to cetch
a grey paraquet and *twift* it
fo as it fqueals aloud
till ye reft of its kind flock round,
therevpon themfelues being cetched);
how there was alfo penguins
(which laft hath but ftumps for wings,
fo being ye eafier to kill)
which we killed above four hundred;
how there was alfo wild geefe
and turtles above an hundred;
how we killed all thefe and more;
and ye Tuefday more and more;
and ye Wednefday more and more;
and ye Thurfday more and more;
ye haue heard this yarn afore.

96

PETER REDGROVE

True Wasp

On the twentieth of this November I noticed
Wasps eating a toad flattened by cars,
Braided to the asphalt, they were tearing away

Strips of leather; later the same day
I saw a dead rat opened by its own gas
With wasps studding its backbone

Like opulent yellow-black brocades,
Epaulettes, medal-ribbons and gliding fruit.
It was their season, turning horror to vigour,

Turning eyes downward; I saw them pinching
Fine ginger crumbs from a reclining dog-turd;
Nipping up tiny blood-and-wood loaves

Off the butcher's sawdust gut-stained floor.
I was caught in our mother the rain,
And still they came weaving through the drops

To seccateur and wing lichen away
In volumes ripped from the bark of my shelter-tree.
They seemed a kind of electrical spark

Attracted by charges; no doubt their helter-skelter flight
Penetrated the power-stations, I wanted to see
Wasps bask in the nesting hum of a dynamo

Dedicated to stinging electricity and painted
Yellow and black for warning. I am sure
They would mulct it of its grease,

With their agility touch down on the shaft
Shining with its spin and lick up
The bland honey of machinery.

CHRISTOPHER REID

Men Against Trees

I note that the deforestation of Brazil
  Is going ahead at a cracking pace.
Valiant feats of giant-toppling! Disgrace
  To the ancient Empire of Chlorophyll!

Nature's strongholds surrender one by one.
  Even here at home, the fight
Continues quietly; men roam about at night
  Snapping saplings – and not just for fun.

Burger boxes and buckled lager cans
  Stuff the guts of older trees.
On more technical missions, auxiliaries
  Steal forth in trucks and vans.

I saw one last week on a daylight job:
  Reversing under the boughs of an ash,
He tore a limb and left an enormous gash.
  You had to admire the insouciant slob!

LAWRENCE SAIL

The Waterbuck

Beyond the corrupt or pure administrations
Where roads run out into dry drifts
The spreading diaspora of the hazy past begins,
Its frontier nothing more than wavy air,
Its guards, *bonzai* thorn-trees deep in rifts:

An Africa of high bleached grasses and blood
With miles of sky and miles of earth
Where every loping landmark has to chance
Its luck across the grey eternal dust,
A passage random as memory or mercy.

But he, intent, remains just where he stood
At the edge of the garbled river, that day –
Neck-high in foliage, garlanded with green,
His soft coat exactly all and none
Of blue and brown and black and mauve and grey.

The waterbuck – his eye also, imperious,
Corrals the light, his horns are already
A trophy held high, his dark muzzle gleams
With refreshing wet, his long collie's face
Is sharp with the taut anticipation of dread.

He kept us fixed, swiftly computed survival,
Dug his weight into the river-bank
And plunged to breast the flood, still self-assertive
And vivid, as he remains. The muddy water
Lapped along the broad gunwales of his flanks.

He has not stood there all these years just waiting
To perform on memory's loop, or trusting
That a poem would occur: now for the first time
I see the accusing simplicity of his claim
For continuance, for nothing more than simple
    justice.

PENELOPE SHUTTLE

Zoo Morning

Elephants prepare to look solemn and move slowly
though all night they drank and danced, partied
and gambled, didn't act their age.

Night-scholar monkeys take off their glasses,
pack away their tomes and theses,
sighing as they get ready for yet another long day
of gibbering and gesticulating, shocking
and scandalizing the punters.

Bears stop shouting their political slogans
and adopt their cute-but-not-really teddies' stance
in the concrete bear-pit.

Big cats hide their flower-presses, embroidery-frames
and water-colours;
grumbling, they try a few practice roars.
Their job is to rend the air, to devour carcasses,
to sleep-lounge at their vicious carnivorous ease.

What a life.
But none of them would give up show-business.

The snakes who are always changing,
skin after skin,
open their aged eyes and hinged jaws in welcome.

Between paddock and enclosure
we drag our unfurred young.
Our speech is over-complex, deceitful.
Our day out is not all it should be.
The kids howl, baffled.

All the animals are very good at being animals.
As usual, we are not up to being us.
Our human smells prison us.

In the insect house
the red-kneed spider dances on her eight light
   fantastics;
on her shelf of silence she waltzes and twirls;
joy in her hairy joints, her ruby-red eyes.

The Little First God

Baal was only a clean slot and a hard shaft
before God complicated men with souls.

The little first-god minted every feisty day
and then he melted down the important hours.
He said he was the new tide and the new wind
which nibbled at beaches and small buntings
but he is as sullen as the woman in labour
whose skirts are full of the darkness of the bloody
    bulging sack.
He was grace and guts and get in the chase
but now he goes churlish into the briar hedge
to look for a ghost to thwack onto the thorns.
He might pick up a peacock's quill
to mask the piebald mantle of his magpie,
but he will have found the woman in the thicket
who horse-rides men with her thighs.

Baal is just the shake of the first coxcomb,
the swing of the thin-fingered boogie-man
playing horse. He is only the long by-word
and the sharp vamp – the swooning girl
    and the seasoned mount.

And he is scarce as feathers on a sparrow's egg.
He is the dregs of the very last half-pint.

MATTHEW SWEENEY

The Eagle

My father is writing in Irish.
The English language, with all its facts
will not do. It is too modern.
It is good for planecrashes, for unemployment,
but not for the unexplained return
of the eagle to Donegal.

He describes the settled pair
in their eyrie on the not-so-high mountain.
He uses an archaic Irish
to describe what used to be, what is again,
though hunters are reluctant
to agree on what will be.

He's coined a new word
for vigilantes who keep a camera watch
on the foothills. He joins them
when he's not writing, and when he is.
He writes about giant eggs,
about a whole new strain.

He brings in folklore
and folk-prophecy. He brings in the date
when the last golden eagle
was glimpsed there. The research is new
and dodgy, but the praise
is as old as the eagle.

PAM THOMPSON

The Last Leaf in the World

My little son
opened the matchbox
cautiously,
just enough for him to see,
his fingers curling around it like tendrils.
I've got the last leaf in the world
he told me,
but I can't show you
because you're too old
and if you look
it will die.

I watched him play;
sunlight freckling his hair;
ridiculous grin, like a fish.
Between us, my great age
and a pane of glass;
on my side a knowledge
of last things,
on his,
a made-up game.

Later, he cried.

That evening, a trespasser,
I crept into his room
to find him hunched in sorrowful sleep
and on the floor,
the matchbox, spilling out
its bits of ash
and tangled bones.

Small blessing
to be glad
that only I
was witness to the light
disappearing from the sky
and the planet,
with its one cold star,
darkening upon betrayal.

ANTHONY THWAITE

Site 792N/57

I

A plastic bag of everything and nothing,
Bulged earth, damp clay, spiked twigs, charcoal,
sogged ash.
Lump heavy as a body. Tip it out,
Let it resolve itself to what it is,
A shovelful of everything and nothing

Crammed where it silted up through centuries,
Now loosed and prised apart and split, rinsed out
In washing-up bowls, stacked and left to dry.
Distinguish it, so each becomes a thing,
Each from its separate silt of centuries:

Here sherds, there glass, here iron, flint, wood, bone,
Waste lead, worked stone. The property of each
Begins to show, comes clear, fit to be named,
Then to be labelled, given provenance:
Thetford or Pingsdorf; tibia, cranium, rib -

Each speaks itself, identified, distinct,
Datable, nameable, however smashed,
However humbled to a rim, a scrap,
Discrete in fragments, now assembled here,
articulates itself, and everything.

II

Deposit, anaerobic: waterlogged,
Free from bacteria, it seems unchanged
Since left there in its burial, prolonged.

Roots absent, but some root-marks visible
On flakings, fissures. Delicate, requires
Careful handling, soft to finger pressures.

Organic, not an artefact. Suggest
Submit to conservation. Drawing shows
Trace-marks recorded. Condition varies.

Age and description multiple, repeated
Within parameters. Volatile condition
Makes difficult a certain recognition.

Retrieved from damp environment, encrusted
In find-spot, still unfractured, held in storage,
This layered thing, or object, defies knowledge.

Put it down, then, *Unrecognisable*:
This is the word usually applicable.

JOHN WHITWORTH

Green Landscape With Small Humans

Sunday in February, and my wife
At the student factory disentangling Shelley's
Bright-patterned whinges on the world and life
And time; one-year-old Katie's filled her wellies
Full of primeval ooze; the morning telly's
Improving or uplifting; Eleanor
Suggests a picnic expedition in the car

To feed dear deers and bunnies at the Wild
Life thingummy and use the trampoline.
Why not? It *is* unseasonably mild
(Probably all that CO_2 between
Here and the weathermaker); points of green
Reclaim our flowerbeds where springtime breeds
Tentative children, snowdrops, crocuses and weeds.

The Garden Centre first for Ellie's poncho
(Left yesterday). This *déjeuner sur l'herbe*'ll
I hope keep all our best behaviours on show.
Now juice and Smarties render us non-verbal
Till Kate drops off and Ellie wants a gerbil.
She gets an ice-cream, just as she'd supposed.
The deers and bunnies place predictably is closed.

Then the seaside's grim arcades and tatty pubs;
A pier the winter gales half swept away
Half lives in lowering, seaweed-bearded stubs
Round whose vast, trunkless legs our children play.
They chase a shrinking sea into Herne Bay
And hoard queer pebbles, shells, coke-cans, wine-corks,
Macdonalds milk-shake tubs and broken plastic forks.

In the dripping shade of these colossal wrecks
Where world's detritus clings like body hair
Two little lives can seem no more than specks
In Time that wastes them to the empty air:
Look on my works, ye mighty, and despair.
Please Daddy, we must save the whales. You pin
This badge on here and put some money in that tin.

The whales were singing on the antique waters
Before our world and life and time began.
Out there they are singing still. Our wandering
    daughters,
Sealed in the fellowship of Leviathan,
Make homeward tracks as slowly as they can.
The lone and level sands are washed with sound
As they sing too: *The wheels of the bus go round and round.*

Peter Blake

JUNIOR SECTION

These are the ten £100-prize-winning poems from the
WWF/*Weekend Guardian* competition. There were three
categories: ages five to eight, nine to fourteen and
fifteen to eighteen. The age of the writer appears at the
head of each poem.

RICHARD HANSEN (aged 16)

Visiting

The immortals are a little despondent tonight
Because they have to visit the Earth,
This Earth that they made and gave over to us.
'It's time to go,'
Shouted Krishna to Christ and uneasy, unhappy,
Silent as moons, they linked arms
And arrived here, here in Brazil,
In the land where we burn trees or fail to succeed.

The immortals are bitter and saddened tonight,
They see we've defiled this altar the Earth.
Krishna and Christ are inclined to forgive,
But Diana demands our instant destruction.
And what about me?
I can't afford to be an ecologist.
How long will I live?
Maybe twenty more years,
I'll be long gone when you choke to death,
Without trees.

The Gods are raging with anger tonight,
The thunder is cracking
Over this dustbowl, these wasted stumps of rain forest
    giants,
This plain, this farm, this home.
And although I can't understand it,
The Gods have said that they're angry with me.

Susan Hedley

ADAM HOROVITZ *(aged 18)*

Tears Like Lava
(clay figures)

Two little people
stand fossilised,
their love frozen
their bodies stone
joined in deathly matrimony,
Siamese by destruction.

They smile at winter,
stare at the sun.
The weather
wears them down,
they stand
crying;
tears like lava.

JEREMY KIDD (aged 16)

Save Us

The moon lies,
a sad memory of the sun.
It drowns in the boatman's oar-ripple.
He contemplates its plight
with silent recognition.
He's left the angry streets,
their vulgar brightness, behind
like a dream best forgotten.
The trees whisper approval to his thoughts
Their sappy soil-and-sky silences
speak with firmness,
'You are right.
     Save us.
Join us.'

TOBY KIDD (aged 11)

Bird in a Winter Garden

The bony skeleton waving,
the white bits falling
to the ground. Somebody
told me the skeletons
are trees, but trees have
leaves. Somebody told me
the bits are snow.
What's snow?

HUGH MARTIN (aged 18)

The Soft-skinned Elephant

An elephant in its entirety lay by the drying pond
Muddied, hoofed a little, sniffed by other elephants
Prodding it
It was a statement; immovable and grey in the heat
Which rose, clung and stank with presence
Nothing was as complete as this tuskless quick-dry
Cemented in, cracked, chapped and full of finished
    purpose
Walked on by white birds pecking who shitted on it
Not understanding
Treated like a rock, so like a rock to them

Throw rocks at it and watch them bounce with a bock
    pock
Slap of stone on skin makes you forget
You can too easily forget it was an animal
He who was an animal reverts to just a stench, an
    obscene bulk
Whose trunk is ridiculous, unnecessary
Covered in a fine white powder
Ivory dusted
Sawed at

They didn't need to say it was hard cooling and dead
To me it remained the soft-skinned elephant.

RACHEL McGILL (aged 15)

Song of a Sizewell Sheep

I'm a lonely sheep
On a Sizewell Hill
And life was a pretty
bitter pill

Until, my darling,
I met you
With your neon eyes
And your fur bright blue

The way you crackle
On a summer's night
Makes me shiver
In sheer delight

And the way your big
Fluorescent eyes
Stare at me
In dumb surprise

Makes me dream
Of a cosy nook
with a Geiger counter
Up on a hook

And a trim little bunker
Shining and neat
And two little lambkins
With twelve little feet.

GEMMA OGDEN (aged 8)

Blue Bells

Blue Bells Cockle Shells
In the river oh, it smells
When the stars come out at Night
Twinkle Twinkle they are bright.

LEE PUNNETT (aged 15)

My Grandfather Speaks

It was old, dark.
The purple and Mahogany
Furniture hard and unyielding wood,
The air choky and
Thick like a blanket.
Tobacco floated about
In long curling rivers
From a pipe resting in an ash tray.
The rustle of movement
Stretched the air.
The low musty voice as
Grandfather speaks.

REBECCA SANDOVER (aged 18)

125

The shrieking arrow cuts the view.
Razor-edged, brutalizing air.
–125–125-
Wheel on track,
sharpening the spiralling consumer.
Under it
nothing is precious,
everything falls
binding me to recur the impact,
choking my sensations.
125, you
rip the horizon's seal,
pour out our howls
which fall upon the smarting ground.
And we are left
committed to attempt repair.

J. WHILEY (aged 17)

Pollution with a Capital 'P'

I'm gonna be a graffiti artist,
I like spraying paint.
It's messy and passes the time.

I spilt oil in the goldfish bowl,
not on purpose, of course.
Mum was upset, said Billy was irreplaceable, who cares?

I lurk in hiding places,
people don't find me till it's too late.
I cause chaos but I'm still here.

Gonna drive a big car.
Get me name in the papers.
Nothing's gonna stop me, they'll have no choice and
    won't ignore me.

I'm five years old,
I'm getting big now,
Mum says me name's pollution.

Mum named me sister Ozone.
Ozone, friendly? Mum says that's a joke.
Can't get it meself, meant to be funny is it?

Mum says Ozone's very holy,
gonna be big and important soon.
Not sure I want a priest as a sister.

I'm six years old,
I'm not taken enough notice of,
me name's pollution.